WUHT

Star Time

ZIGZAG KIDS

PATRICIA REILLY GIFF

Star Time

illustrated by

ALASDAIR BRIGHT

WENDY
LAMB
BOOKS

Text copyright © 2011 by Patricia Reilly Giff
Jacket art and interior illustrations copyright © 2011 by Alasdair Bright

All rights reserved. Published in the United States by Wendy Lamb Books,
an imprint of Random House Children's Books,
a division of Random House, Inc., New York.
Wendy Lamb Books and the colophon are trademarks
of Random House, Inc.

ISBN 978-0-385-73888-0

Printed at Berryville Graphics
Berryville, VA
November 2011

Random House Children's Books supports the First Amendment and
celebrates the right to read.

Love to Alice,
my Number One Girl
—P.R.G.

Big thanks to Carolyn LaFontaine,
whose book started me illustrating!
—A.B.

Yolanda

Sumiko

Charlie

Destiny

Gina

Mitchell

Habib

Clifton

Trevor

Beebe

Angel

Peter

CHAPTER 1

FRIDAY

Great days at the Zigzag Afternoon Center!

They were going to do a play.

Gina would be the star. She was sure of it. She'd told everyone she knew.

She ducked into the girls' room. She held Destiny Washington's bottle of Curls Galore gel.

Destiny had lent it to her yesterday. "I'm trying to be the nicest person," she had said.

"Even to kids who don't deserve it. Stars do that."

Today Gina was wearing her star shirt. Best of all, she had on Grandma Maroni's loopy pearls. They hung down almost to her knees.

It was all because a used-to-be-famous actress was coming to the Center. Maybe in a limousine. Her name was Madam Ballantine.

She was going to tell them about acting.

Gina knew that part already.

She was going to talk about stars, too. That was what Gina wanted to hear.

"Mi-mi-mi," Gina sang to herself. She'd never been a star. Not once in her whole life. But maybe this time . . .

She opened Destiny's bottle of gel. It was a little sticky. It was blue.

How much should she use?

She held it up. The gel was thick and bubbly.

She shook it over the top of her head. Nothing poured out.

Then came a little bloop.

The rest of it came in a big galump.

It slithered over her hair and down her front. A long bubbly blue drip on her star shirt!

She scrubbed at it with a paper towel.

It wasn't a drip anymore. It looked like a bird with wings.

Gina swallowed. Maybe Destiny had her sparkly purse today. If only she'd lend her that, too.

Gina could hold it exactly over the bird spot.

She scrunched up her hair the way Destiny had told her. Sticky but cool.

She headed for the lunchroom.

A million kids were there, screeching and screaming. It was snack time: fried mozzarella sticks today.

Gina slid into the seat across from Sumiko.
Sumiko was looking at her hair. Or maybe it was the bird-with-wings drip. Then Sumiko looked away.

Sumiko was a polite girl. Even Mrs. Farelli, the tough art teacher, said so.

"Don't you love Afternoon Center?" Sumiko asked. "The snacks are great."

Gina touched the top of her head. She took a bite of the mozzarella stick. It felt like her hair. Gooey.

Beebe leaned closer. Sometimes it was hard for her to hear. "The play will be exciting, too," she said.

"Beebe's right!" Gina said. Her heart thumped.

She *had* to be the star.

She'd told Grandma Maroni. And Aunt Suki. And Uncle Tony. She closed her eyes. Who else? Everyone on her block. Even the meat man at Stop & Shop. They were all coming to see her.

She had to look like a star.

"Have you seen Destiny?" she asked Sumiko.

"She's around somewhere," Sumiko said. "Her hair is gorgeous. It's swooped up with a purple bow."

"Nice." Gina crossed her fingers.

"The bow has a diamond in the middle," Sumiko said.

"Very nice." Gina tried to cross her toes.

"And . . ." Beebe leaned forward. "She's wearing a fat purple ring."

Gina didn't say anything. She had nothing left to cross.

That Destiny was so lucky. Her mom was a hairdresser. Gina's own mom just hung around and drew Happy-Birthday-to-You cards.

Destiny looked like a star with her swooped-up-purple-diamond-bow hair.

Gina was ready to cry. Too bad she was such a loud crier. Loud as a hyena, Destiny had said once.

Gina had to get out of there before her crying began. "See you," she told Sumiko and Beebe.

She went up the stairs.

No one was supposed to be in the classrooms during Afternoon Center. But just this once.

Somebody else was up there, too. Charlie was running along the hall. He was taking little hops. His yellow rain-coat flapped behind him.

Gina forgot

about crying. Charlie was fun. He was an inventor. "What are you doing?" she asked.

"It's my Yellow Wing-O invention," he said. "I'm learning to fly."

"Wow. Good luck," Gina said.

She opened her classroom door. It was quiet in there. No kids. No teacher.

Gina looked at her desk. It was a little messy. Books and papers were half in, half out.

She took a step toward Ms. Katz's desk. The teacher's desk was even worse than hers.

She told herself not to look. Ms. Katz's stuff was private.

She couldn't help seeing Destiny Washington's math paper. There were cross-outs all over it.

Destiny's paper was the biggest mess in the room. Gina's paper was poking out, too. *Very good,* it said. *Just a little sloppy.*

Cool.

She heard a huge *clump* out in the hall. Then "Oof."

Charlie must have crashed.

There was a mirror in Ms. Katz's closet. It was all right to look at that. Mirrors weren't private.

She stood on tiptoe to see her whole self.

Would the used-to-be-famous actress like a girl with a bird-with-wings spot on her shirt?

The bird-with-wings had grown. Now it looked like a hippopotamus.

She was getting worried. Her heart thumped.

"Get your act together," she whispered to herself. That was what Mrs. Farelli always said.

Gina opened her mouth wide. "Do, re, mi-mi-

mi . . ." Lovely. Loud and clear, even with a thumping heart.

"I am going to be the star," she sang.

If only Destiny would lend her that sparkly purse to cover the hippopotamus/bird-with-wings.

CHAPTER 2

STILL FRIDAY

Gina poked her head into the art room.

Destiny wasn't there.

She opened the gym door next.

Clunk! A basketball hit her in the head. She tossed it back.

"Ew," Habib said. "It has goo all over it."

Gina gulped. She opened the girls' room door. She heard a voice. A strange, wiggly voice.

"I've come from a planet far away," it said.

Gina jumped back.

Something had invaded the school.

Slowly she poked her head around the door.

"Destiny Washington!" she said.

"Just practicing," Destiny said. "That's what stars do." She stopped. "What happened to your shirt?"

Gina raised one shoulder. "Could I borrow your purse for tryouts?"

"My best purse, with the sparkly front and the striped back?" Destiny began to shake her head.

"I have to cover this stain."

Destiny leaned closer. "It looks like a—what's that thing with a horn on its head?"

"A rhinoceros?" Gina leaned forward. "I'll be your best friend forever."

Destiny rolled Chap Stick over her mouth. She smacked her lips together. "I guess so. Here"

Gina held up the purse. Yes. It covered most of her shirt. Only the rhino's horn hung out. Or maybe it was the hippo's tail.

They headed for the auditorium. Kids were all over the hall.

Habib was juggling a mozzarella stick.

Angel was jumping rope without a rope.

Angel's friend Yolanda was Irish step dancing. Her shoes were clinking and clanking.

Click! Click!

Suddenly everything was still. No one moved. There wasn't a sound in the hall.

Mrs. Farelli was snapping her fingers. She was the world's best snapper.

Her snap meant: "Quiet!"

After a moment, everyone began to walk on tiptoe.

In the auditorium, Peter Petway and Mitchell McCabe were lying on the floor. Papers were spread out around them.

They were working on the play: *A Robot World*.

Peter was writing.

Mitchell was thinking.

The play was about a wild space station. Bad guys were all over the place. Too bad. Gina had been hoping for princesses, and frogs turning into princes.

She would have made a great princess.

Charlie would have made a great frog.

Now everyone ran to the window. Gina looked over Destiny's shoulder.

A car had pulled up in front of the school.

It was an old car, a clunker.

It was the actress, Madam Ballantine!

She came up the walk. She was skinny as a pretzel stick. Her hair was a mess. Too bad she didn't have any of Destiny's Curls Galore gel.

Madam Ballantine came into the auditorium.

"We're doing aliens and comets crashing," Peter said.

"Wonderful." Madam Ballantine looked around. "I hope you'll all come to my play on Tuesday. It's at the Star Theater."

"Of course," said Mrs. Farelli.

"Of course," Gina said, too. She stepped a little bit in front of Destiny. She wanted to be sure the actress saw her. She looped up Grandma Maroni's pearls.

Destiny gave her a push. "You're taking up my airspace."

Gina pushed back.

"Hey!" Destiny yelled. "No pushing at the Zigzag School." She grabbed her sparkly purse away from Gina.

Gina tried to grab it back.

What would the used-to-be-famous Madam Ballantine think of a girl with a hippo-bird on her shirt? Or a rhino?

Mrs. Farelli came toward them. "Outside," she said. "Both of you."

They followed Mrs. Farelli into the hall. *Everyone must be staring,* Gina thought. She looked down at her sneakers.

"This is a fine kettle of fish," Mrs. Farelli

said. "What must Madam Ballantine think?"

"Sorry," Gina said.

"Sorry," Destiny said, too.

"Sit out here for a while," Mrs. Farelli said. "Get your act together."

Mrs. Farelli disappeared back into the auditorium.

Gina and Destiny slid down against the wall. They watched a bunch of kids go inside.

Four girls said they were going to be stars.

Four boys said they were going to be robots.

"How long do you think we have to sit here?" Gina asked.

"Maybe for the rest of the afternoon," Destiny said.

"But what about the actress?" Gina hoped she wasn't going to cry like a hyena.

This afternoon wasn't turning out very well.

Not very well at all.

CHAPTER 3

TOO BAD—IT'S STILL FRIDAY

Outside, Gina could hear the *slap-slap* of a jump rope.

Inside, she heard voices. "SOMETHING IS WRONG WITH THIS SPACESHIP!" someone shouted.

That was Mitchell.

"He must be reading part of the play," Destiny said.

"A nice loud voice," Madam Ballantine said.

Gina peered through the crack in the door. "Do you think Mrs. Farelli forgot about us?"

The gym door opened.

Mrs. Farelli came out. She kept going down the hall.

A moment later, she was gone.

"Maybe she's going home," Destiny said. "I guess we'll be here all night."

"With nothing to eat?" Gina asked. Her mother would be sad. Mom wanted her to have good healthy food.

"Maybe they turn off the heat at night," Destiny said. "We may freeze."

Gina held on to Grandma Maroni's pearls. She could see blocks of ice in the hall. Icicles on the ceiling!

"There's something worse," Destiny said. "Today is Friday. We may be here for the whole weekend."

Gina opened her mouth. A sound came out.

"Are you going to cry like a hyena?" Destiny asked.

Gina snapped her mouth shut. The hyena was trapped inside her throat.

In the auditorium, Mitchell was yelling again. "WATCH OUT! THE SPACESHIP IS GOING TO CRASH!"

"Bloop. Bloop. Bloop," said Peter.

"Wow," said Madam Ballantine.

"I guess that's the spaceship crashing." Destiny stood up. "I'm going in there."

"You can't do that," Gina said.

"Mrs. Farelli wouldn't want us to freeze to death. I think she just forgot about us." Destiny banged open the auditorium door.

She went inside.

Gina thought about going inside, too. But suppose Mrs. Farelli came back?

She put her head against the wall.

Tonight her mother was making turkey with stuffing.

No dinner for her.

And bedtime was nine o'clock.

Would she still be here? Sleeping on the hall floor like a frozen ant?

"I WILL SAVE YOU," someone said in a loud voice.

Thank goodness, Gina thought. Then she realized. It was Destiny. She was trying to be the star.

Poor Grandma Maroni. Poor Aunt Suki and Uncle Tony. Poor meat man at Stop & Shop. What would they think if they heard Gina wasn't a star?

She yanked on the pearls.

Snap!

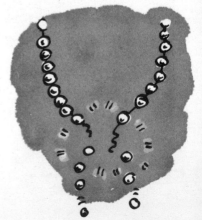

They flew all over the place.

The hyena was escaping from her throat. She couldn't stop it.

She began to cry.

Someone opened the auditorium door. It was Clifton, a kindergarten kid. "You sound like a—" he began.

Gina gulped. She hoped he wouldn't say *hyena*.

He didn't. "You sound like a sad girl," he said.

That made her cry even louder.

Jake the Sweeper popped his head around the stairs. He swept some pearls toward her. "What's going on?" he asked.

Now everyone came out of the auditorium. They crowded around her.

Gina squinched her eyes shut.

"What's this?" a soft voice asked.

She opened her eyes again.

The used-to-be-famous actress was staring at her.

Gina knew she was a mess. Her hair was gooey. She looked down. Her shirt had . . . not a hippo, not a rhino, but—

A pair of elephants.

How had that happened?

"Perfect," the used-to-be-famous actress said.

Gina wiped her eyes.

"You can be a poor lost alien in the play," the actress said.

Gina stood up. "Is that the star?"

The actress shook her head. "No, but it would be a lovely part. All you'd have to do is cry."

"Not the star?" Gina said.

"Well—" said Madam Ballantine.

"I'll be the star," said Destiny.

"What about me?" Beebe said.

Mrs. Farelli came along the hall. "What is all this commotion?"

"I don't want to stay out here forever," Gina told her.

"I forgot." Mrs. Farelli slapped her forehead. "I'm so sorry."

Whew!

Outside, Ramón, the college helper, blew his whistle. "Time to get on the bus," he said.

"Hurry," Madam Ballantine said. "See you on Tuesday."

Gina stopped to pick up some of the pearls. She put them in her pocket. Poor Grandma Maroni. What would she say?

But Grandpa Maroni could fix anything.

Maybe he could even fix the necklace.

She raced up the stairs. She'd have turkey with stuffing for supper. She'd sleep in her own bed.

She waved goodbye to Mrs. Farelli and to Madam Ballantine.

She'd worry about being a crybaby alien next week.

CHAPTER 4

MONDAY

Gina and Destiny looked in the auditorium.

"No play practice today," Mitchell said. "Jake the Sweeper is painting the walls."

"Tan," said Destiny. "Yuck."

"A lovely color," Mrs. Farelli said behind them.

Yuck, Gina thought. "Lovely," she said. Stars were kind.

25

Mrs. Farelli tilted her head. "I have a dress the same color as the wall. I'll wear it to Madam Ballantine's play tomorrow."

"Lovely," Gina said again.

"Lovely," Destiny said at the same time.

Too bad Destiny's voice was louder than hers.

Gina headed for the music room. She hadn't been there for a few days. Mr. Sarsaparilla, the music teacher, must miss her. After all, she was going to be an opera singer when she grew up.

She passed the gym. Charlie had a bandage on his nose.

"From your Yellow Wing-O invention?" Gina asked.

Charlie shook his head. "From my Walk-on-a-Rope-O invention." He looked a little sad. "The rope-o broke-o."

Gina knew how he felt. Suppose she turned out to be a crybaby alien instead of the star?

She went into the music room.

Mr. Sarsaparilla was banging on his drums. He was banging a mile a minute. His hair was flying, his feet were jumping.

He was singing something.

Gina tapped her foot.

She began to sing. She sang loudly. Her notes got higher as she went along. It was lovely. "OOH-LA-LA."

Mr. Sarsaparilla jumped. His drumsticks crashed. "Oh, Yolanda," he said. "It's you."

Gina shook her head.

"I mean Destiny," he said.

"I'm Gina, the opera singer," she told him.

He pulled on his long, sweeping mustache. "Right. The loudest singer in the Afternoon Center."

Gina looked around. No one else was in the music room. Poor Mr. Sarsaparilla was in there all by himself.

"I liked your song," she said, "about—" She couldn't remember what it was about.

"It's called 'You Can Do Almost Anything,'" Mr. Sarsaparilla said.

"Is that true?" Gina said.

Mr. Sarsaparilla banged his drum with his stick. "Yes indeed."

An idea popped into her head.

She could do something!

She could be the star.

She could help Mr. Sarsaparilla, too.

The audience would be clapping. She could see them!

The meat man at Stop & Shop would give her a slice of bologna.

"The Afternoon Center is putting on a play," she told Mr. Sarsaparilla.

"Enchanting," he said.

Sometimes Mr. Sarsaparilla didn't talk regular English.

"Not one singer in the whole thing," she

said. "It's about a bunch of robots, and bad guys, and crying aliens."

"Unfortunate," said Mr. Sarsaparilla.

Gina pointed to herself. "We could use some opera in there."

Mr. Sarsaparilla yanked on his mustache again. "I don't think—" he began.

"And drums," she said. "Lots of nice banging drums."

Mr. Sarsaparilla yanked harder. "But I'm the only one who plays the drums."

"Yes," Gina said. "It's lucky. Peter and Mitchell are my friends. They might give you a good part."

He looked up at the ceiling. "Teaching music is not easy," he whispered.

Gina smiled. She was so glad she'd thought of this. Mr. Sarsaparilla might never have been a star in his whole life.

She skipped out of the music room. She sang, "You can do almost anything, tra-la." She sang it under her breath.

Everyone didn't have to know about it just yet.

CHAPTER 5

STILL MONDAY

Gina went to find Mitchell. She sang all the way down the hall.

She'd have to do something about her hair.

How could she be a star with straight-as-a-string hair? If only she hadn't used up all of Destiny's Curls Galore gel.

She thought of Grandma Maroni's loopy pearls. It made her sad.

But Grandma Maroni said she didn't mind. "I have a drawerful of look-like-real jewels," she said.

Gina threw open the gym door.

"ROBOTS-AND-SPACESHIPS-OH-MY," she sang.

Beebe stopped hopping on one foot. She stared at Gina.

Sumiko stopped swinging on the gym rope. She slid to the floor.

Charlie was on top of the bleachers. He looked surprised. He probably thought she was a star singer.

Destiny was in the corner. She was waving her arms around. She was talking to herself. But now she stopped. Her mouth was open.

Gina nodded. Everyone in the gym was staring at her. It was her singing, of course.

Too bad about today's shirt. It had a teeny-but-you-could-still-see-it noodle soup spot.

Peter was leaning against the back of a chair. He had a notepad in his hand.

Mitchell was lying on the floor. His legs were wiggling around in the air. He looked like a skinny spider. "What next?" he was saying.

Gina thought of Mr. Sarsaparilla again. *You can do almost anything.*

She sank down next to them.

She peered at the notepad.

Cross-outs all over the place.

"Erasers are helpful," she said in a Ms. Katz voice.

She said it kindly.

"It's our sloppy copy," Peter said. "We have to add another bad guy. My brother, Trevor, wants a part."

"That's just what I wanted to talk to you about," Gina said. "I'm here to help."

"No thanks," Peter and Mitchell said together.

They might turn out to be difficult boys, Gina thought.

"Madam Ballantine might want a girl writer, too," she said.

Mitchell frowned. "I didn't hear her say that."

"Me neither," said Peter.

"Really?" Gina said. It was the perfect answer. Not a lie.

Mitchell filled his mouth with air. He puffed out one cheek. Then he puffed out the other. "We can ask her tomorrow."

"Maybe we shouldn't bother her," Gina said.

Clifton, Trevor's best friend, slid up to them. "How come I'm not in this play?" he asked.

Mitchell stopped puffing. "We'll add another bad guy."

"I want to be a robot," Clifton said.

Mitchell sighed. "We have a zillion robots."

"One more won't hurt," Gina said.

"All right," Mitchell said.

She sat back. She was getting nicer by the minute. And helpful!

Clifton slid away.

"You don't have any opera stars," Gina said.

"This is a space story." Mitchell began to puff again.

Gina frowned. "I bet you don't have one crashing drummer."

"You think there are drummers in outer space?" Peter asked.

He sounded like her father when his socks got all mixed up, she thought. "Don't worry. We're going to do this together. It will be . . ."

She tried to think of the word Mr. Sarsaparilla had used.

"Enchanting," she said at last.

Peter began to shake his head.

Mitchell puffed out his cheek one more time. "We'll think about it."

"Think hard," she said.

CHAPTER 6

TUESDAY—FIELD TRIP DAY

Bus Thirteen pulled up in front of the Afternoon Center. It was the worst one. It always had smoke coming out the back.

Gina was out the door. She walked right behind Mrs. Farelli in her auditorium-colored dress.

Today they were going to see Madam Ballantine in her play.

It would be a long ride. They were having snacks on the way. Purple yogurt.

Gina carried her mother's huge purple purse. Just in case! It would cover every single yogurt dot.

It had a bunch of other things, too:

A writing pad for helping Peter and Mitchell.

A pencil with the sharpest point in the world.

A brand-new eraser that smelled like orange juice.

And a dollar for just-in-case.

Destiny rushed past. Gina knew she wanted to sit next to the bus driver. It was the woman who looked just like Charlie.

Charlie came along next. He was carrying a paper bag. It was dripping a little.

"It's for my Wet-O Dry-O invention," he said. "I want to see how long it takes for water to disappear."

Gina stepped back so Sumiko could go next.

"Thanks," Sumiko said.

"Don't worry," Gina said. "I'm waiting for Peter and Mitchell."

Mitchell was last.

That made her last, too.

"Where's Peter?" she asked.

"Home with double earaches," Mitchell said.

They had to sit in seats at the back. Not a great spot.

Very bumpy for the yogurt!

But never mind that.

"Did you think hard?" she asked Mitchell.

Mitchell didn't answer. He was trying to balance his yogurt on his writing-the-play pad.

Gina pointed to the pad. What a mess it was, with those cross-outs. There was a big rip down the middle, too.

Mitchell took a huge spoonful of yogurt.

She almost said, "Watch out!" But it was too late.

Yogurt dripped on Mitchell's shirt and jeans. Even his chin was purple.

The bus lurched.

A huge glump of yogurt landed on Gina's knee. It was wet; it was cold. All because of Bus Thirteen.

It was a good thing she had the purse.

"Yeow!" Charlie yelled. "My Wet-O Dry-O invention is all over the floor."

"I knew it," the driver said.

The bus bumped up to the curb. "Hold on,

everyone!" the driver yelled. The bus rolled to a stop. "This bus is trouble."

"Oh, no," Destiny said. "We're going to miss the play."

Gina looked down at the writing-the-play pad. It was filled with little purple yogurt blobs.

"Don't worry," the driver said. "Another bus will be along soon." She began to sing. "Row, row, row your boat . . ."

The driver was right. In a few minutes, Bus Eight came along.

It was the best one.

Everyone began to rush off Bus Thirteen. Quickly Gina stuck her mostly empty yogurt cup into her purse.

"Want me to put your write-the-play pad in my purse, too?" Gina asked Mitchell. "Plenty of room."

"Good idea," Mitchell said.

They climbed onto the new bus.

Gina made sure to hold the purse over her yogurt-splatted pants.

And then they were at the door of the Star Theater.

"Hurry," said Mrs. Farelli.

Inside, it was dark. Gina didn't have to worry about yogurt stains and huge purses.

She'd talk to Mitchell about the play later.

She sank down into the plushy seat.

A moment later, the curtain started to rise.

The play was ready to begin.

CHAPTER 7

STILL TUESDAY

Gina sat between Mitchell and Destiny. Her purse was smushed against her knees.

She looked at the huge blue curtain in front. It looked like velvet.

The dark was like velvet, too.

Gina loved it.

The curtain was still rising slowly. Everyone began to clap.

Onstage was a big black cat.

The cat didn't pay attention to the clapping. Instead, it held one round paw up to its whiskers.

Slowly it washed one ear.

It waved its curved tail.

It was almost as if the cat were real. It acted like Grandma Maroni's cat.

Soon a girl came out onto the stage. She wore a long dress. It had green look-like-real diamonds on it. It had roses down the front.

It was gorgeous.

The girl was singing a little. "Tra-la." She had flowers in her hand.

Gina leaned over. She whispered to Mitchell, "See. It's good to have singing."

This is a perfect play, Gina thought. *It is about a princess and a frog.*

The cat reached out with one paw.

Would it catch the frog?

Gina took a deep breath. Poor frog.

But the cat sat back. It licked its paw.

It seemed as if the cat were smiling.

But Gina knew what would come next. The star would kiss the frog.

The frog would turn into a prince.

And that was just what happened.

The cat closed its eyes and yawned.

The curtain came down. The lights came on.

Everyone clapped for a long time.

It was time to ask Mitchell again. "Did you have time to think hard?"

"I guess Peter and I can do it alone."

"Maybe not," she said.

"Mrs. Farelli says I'm a good writer," Mitchell said.

"You're the best," Gina said, before she had time to think.

The stars came to the front of the stage.

They all bowed.

The cat took off its mask.

Gina drew in her breath. It was Madam Ballantine.

What a surprise!

It was time to get back on the bus. They had to hurry.

"Oh, dear," said Mrs. Farelli. "It's Bus Thirteen again."

The bus driver turned on the motor.

Nothing happened.

"I knew it," Destiny said. "We'll be here until midnight. We'll be starving."

Gina didn't care how long it took to get home. She needed time to talk to Mitchell—

To beg Mitchell.

Besides, there was still a little purple yogurt left in her purse. She might be hungry, but she wouldn't starve.

She followed Mitchell to the back of the bus.

She passed Charlie. "I might grow some frogs in a tank," he was saying.

"That's not a neat idea at all," the bus driver said.

Sumiko was doing a handstand on the seat.

It was a good thing Mrs. Farelli didn't see her. Mrs. Farelli's head was stuck under the hood of the bus.

The used-to-be-famous actress came outside. She was smiling at everyone.

Too bad her hair was a mess.

Gina poked her head out a window. "You were the best cat in the world," she said.

"That's what acting is all about," the actress

said. "I'm a great cat." She gave a little hop. "I'm working on being a frog."

Gina shook her head. "Frogs aren't easy."

There was a rumble from the bus.

Mrs. Farelli had fixed the problem. She jumped back on the bus.

Her auditorium-colored dress was engine-colored now.

There was a roar and some smoke.

They pulled away from the curb.

The actress waved after them.

"Whew," said Mitchell. "I didn't want to stay here until midnight. I'm hungry already."

"I'll share my yogurt," Gina said.

She reached into her purse.

Everything inside was gooey.

It felt like Destiny's Curls Galore gel. It wasn't, though.

It was the rest of her yogurt.

It had dripped onto her pencil, her paper, her just-in-case dollar.

Mitchell was watching.

She pulled out his play-writing pad.

It was covered with yogurt.

Mitchell tried to wipe it off.

"I can't read one word," Gina said.

"Me neither," Mitchell said. "I'll have to start over."

"I'm sorry," Gina said. "I'm really—"

Mitchell rubbed his hands on his shirt. "I just changed my mind," he said. "You can help."

"Enchanting," she said.

CHAPTER 8

WEDNESDAY

Gina sat on the edge of the Afternoon Center stage.

It was like the one at the Star Theater. So was the soft blue curtain.

It made her think of Madam Ballantine.

She remembered the actress's black cat costume and her round black paws.

Gina swung her legs back and forth. It was

nice to be up there alone with all those empty seats.

In a couple of days, they'd be filled.

The audience would clap. They'd yell "Olé!" For her!

Gina stopped to think. *Olé* was for bullfighting. Maybe they'd yell "Bravo!"

"Yes, that's it," she told herself in a star voice.

Something bumped behind the curtain. Was someone back there?

Yes. The thing was laughing. It had a weird voice. It cackled like a witch.

Maybe it *was* a witch!

But no. It was worse.

"I have come to take you to my planet," the voice said.

Gina's mouth went dry. She didn't want to go to another planet. Her mother was baking ravioli for dinner. Grandma and Grandpa Maroni were coming.

Too bad Grandpa couldn't fix the pearls. It was a good thing Grandma was bringing another set.

Gina opened her mouth. Out came a hyena cry.

"Yeow, there's an animal out there!" the thing yelled.

It sounded a little like an alien.

Or maybe like Destiny.

The back door of the stage slammed shut.

The thing was gone.

But what about the animal?

Gina jumped off the stage. It might be a big one with curved teeth.

Maybe it had escaped from the zoo in Bridgeport.

The auditorium door banged open. Peter raced in.

Mitchell raced in behind him.

"I have paper!" Peter yelled. "I have a pen. We have to write this thing in two seconds."

Gina took a quick look around.

No animal.

No alien.

They sat in the front row.

Peter began to write: *A ROBOT WORLD*.

"I have lots of ideas," Gina told them.

Peter looked at her. "What are you doing here?"

"Mitchell said I could."

Peter sighed. "You'd better have fast ideas. Madam Ballantine is coming."

Mitchell looked sad. "I don't even have time for snack in the lunchroom today."

"I checked," Gina said. "It's leftover soup with red things."

"Whew," Mitchell said. "That's the worst."

"Listen," she said. "Mr. Sarsaparilla could do a whole thing with drums. DUM-DA-DA-DUM."

Peter shook his head. "We need aliens and a spaceship. Everyone is counting on that."

"And don't forget the crybaby alien," said Mitchell.

Gina didn't want to think about that. She took a breath. "We need a star, too."

"That's what Madam Ballantine said," Mitchell told them.

Gina sat back. This was easier than she'd thought. "I was thinking," she began slowly. "The star could be the princess of a planet."

"Yes." Peter began to write.

Gina crossed her fingers. Here came the hard part.

"There could be a robot frog," she said. "The princess could kiss the frog."

Mitchell looked up for a second. "This is like the play we saw."

Gina nodded. "Then the frog turns into—"

"Perfect," Peter said. "The frog turns into an alien. It eats the whole planet."

"Maybe the princess's leg, too," said Mitchell.

"Wait a minute," Gina said. "It's a nice frog."

Peter and Mitchell looked at her.

"Well," she said, "it could be a bad frog. But the princess has to save the planet."

The auditorium door opened again. Kids were coming now.

Madam Ballantine was at the door.

"Put me in for the princess," Gina said. "Hurry."

"But who'll be the crybaby alien?" Peter asked.

The auditorium door opened again.

It was Destiny. She wore a silver outfit from Halloween. She had a gold crown on her head.

"I have come to take you to my planet," she said.

"My," said Madam Ballantine.

Poor Destiny. She thought she was going to be the star. But she was going to be the crybaby alien.

"Unfortunate," Gina said in a Mr. Sarsaparilla voice.

CHAPTER 9

THURSDAY

The bell rang. It was time for Afternoon Center.

Gina pounded down the stairs.

Everyone else pounded, too.

There was just enough time for a snack.

Gina was first in the lunchroom.

The lunchroom lady's face was red. "Whew." She wiped her forehead. "I'm trying to make gingersnaps."

"Great," Gina said.

"I'm still working on them," the lunchroom lady said. "But for today we'll have cheese poppers. It's what I do best."

Gina saw Destiny come into the lunchroom.

Destiny was the lunchroom lady's helper. She put a pile of poppers on a plate.

She had tears in her eyes.

Maybe she was practicing to be the crybaby alien.

Too bad Destiny couldn't cry like a hyena.

Gina sat at a back table. Trevor sat there, too.

"I'm a bad guy in the play." He made a horrible face. He held his hands out like claws.

He wiped popper crumbs off his face. "I'm good at that, right? I like to scare my little sister."

Gina put the last of the poppers in her mouth. She had worked on being a star last night.

She'd stood in front of the mirror.

"I am the princess. I'm going to save the planet," she'd said.

She'd said it a hundred times.

A thousand times.

She still sounded like Gina.

Too bad. Grandma Maroni was going to let Gina wear her second-best loopy pearls.

Gina was going to wear Mom's silver slippers. They'd be stuffed with paper. That way they'd fit. Almost.

Mitchell slid into the seat next to her.

"What are you going to be in the play?" Gina asked. "I can't remember."

Mitchell shook his head. "I'm a writer, not an alien. I might try for bad guy in the next play." He jammed a popper in his mouth. "I have to work on it."

Destiny came to their table. She had a new bottle of Curls Galore gel.

She held it out to Gina. "Since you're going to be the star."

"Thank you," Gina said.

She could see that Destiny was still crying a little.

Gina felt like crying, too. She didn't know why. She stood up. She waved the Curls Galore gel around. "See you guys later." She could hardly get the words out.

Gina went upstairs to the classroom.

No one would be there. It would be nice and quiet.

She had to figure something out.

Why was she ready to cry like a hyena?

All the way upstairs, she thought about Madam Ballantine. She had looked just like a black cat.

The actress had said she was a great cat.

That was true, Gina thought.

Madam Ballantine had had the best part in that play.

A cat!

Gina thought of the long dress she was going to wear. She thought about Grandma Maroni's pearls.

She looked at her feet. Mom's silver shoes would look—

What was that word?

Enchanting.

Gina began to cry.

A hyena cry. No, a crybaby alien cry.

She knew what she had to do. It would be hard. But it was the right thing.

CHAPTER 10

TWO FRIDAYS LATER

At last it was the day of the play.

Gina wore a lime-green costume. It was huge.

The sleeves covered her hands. The skirt dragged along the floor.

She looked like a turtle with no neck.

Mrs. Farelli had found it for her.

It was horrible.

Never mind. She had to look like a crybaby alien.

Besides, she was wearing Mom's silver slippers.

Gorgeous.

Mom thought aliens might wear shoes like that. "No one really knows," she'd said.

Underneath her costume, Gina wore Grandma Maroni's second-best loopy pearls. They hung down to her knees.

Gorgeous, too, even though no one could see them.

She peeked through the curtain.

Everyone was there. Even the meat man from Stop & Shop. And Grandma and Grandpa Maroni. Grandma wore her third-best loopy pearls.

"Shhh, everyone," Mrs. Farelli whispered.

Her whispering was loud. The whole audience could hear her.

Destiny began to laugh. Gina felt a little like laughing, too.

She didn't, though.

The play had to be perfect.

Mitchell swished open the curtain.

Charlie was sitting in a spaceship. It still looked like an old box with wheels.

"We're going to crash into a planet!" Charlie yelled.

A wheel fell off the spaceship.

Great. They hadn't even practiced that.

A bunch of robots marched across the stage. They wore cardboard boxes covered in silver paper.

Now Gina opened her mouth. She opened it wide.

She began to cry like a hyena.

Grandma Maroni gasped. So did the meat man.

Her mother and father didn't. They were used to the hyena crying. Besides, she'd been practicing.

She cried every two minutes. Even when she wasn't sad.

In the front row, Madam Ballantine was smiling.

Gina looked across at Destiny, the star. Destiny looked like a star. She sounded like a star.

For a minute, Gina was sorry she wasn't the one wearing a beautiful gown.

But only for a minute.

She was a great crier.

And there was that surprise at the end. She and Mitchell and Peter had figured it out just yesterday.

But right now, Charlie was being turned into a hopping frog.

Gina had to run away from him.

Too bad her costume was so long. She tried to hold it up.

No good.

She tripped across the stage.

She landed on the spaceship. The other wheel fell off. It rolled away.

Grandma Maroni's pearls shot out all over the place.

Then she was really crying like a hyena!

What would the meat man think?

And poor Grandma Maroni. Her second-best loopy pearls were ruined.

Gina took a peek at the audience. Everyone was sitting forward.

They thought it was all part of the play. Even Madam Ballantine. She winked at Gina.

It was time for Destiny to tackle the frog.

"Oof!" Charlie yelled.

"I have saved the planet," Destiny said.

The curtain closed, and everyone clapped. No one heard Destiny slide over a pearl.

"Don't worry," Mitchell said. "We'll pick up all the pearls later."

Destiny gave Gina a hug. "You're a star crier," she said.

Gina hugged back. "You were great, too."

Then came the surprise.

There was the sound of the drums. *DUM-DUM-DE-DUM!*

It was Mr. Sarsaparilla, star drummer.

Beebe pulled back the curtain. Gina stepped out in front. She opened her mouth.

This time she wasn't crying. She was singing.

Opera singing.

"YOU CAN DO ALMOST ANYTHING, TRA-LA, TRA-LA . . ."

Everyone was smiling. *Whew,* Gina thought.

She was good at something. Not great. But good was enough.

In the back, Mrs. Farelli was whispering again. "This is the best play we've ever had."

Gina thought so, too.

She finished her song. She hated for the play to end.

She sang her song all over again. She was some star!

Enchanting!

PATRICIA REILLY GIFF is the author of many beloved books for children, including the Kids of the Polk Street School books, the Friends and Amigos books, and the Polka Dot Private Eye books. Several of her novels for older readers have been chosen as ALA-ALSC Notable Children's Books and ALA-YALSA Best Books for Young Adults. They include *The Gift of the Pirate Queen; All the Way Home; Water Street; Nory Ryan's Song,* a Society of Children's Book Writers and Illustrators Golden Kite Honor Book for Fiction; and the Newbery Honor Books *Lily's Crossing* and *Pictures of Hollis Woods. Lily's Crossing* was also chosen as a *Boston Globe–Horn Book* Honor Book. Her most recent books for older readers include *Storyteller, Wild Girl,* and *Eleven.* Other books in the Zigzag Kids series include *Number One Kid, Big Whopper,* and *Flying Feet.* Patricia Reilly Giff lives in Connecticut.

ALASDAIR BRIGHT is a freelance illustrator who has worked on numerous books and advertising projects. He loves drawing and is never without his sketchbook. He lives in Bedford, England.